To Garrett
For His Birthday 1997
From Grandmother Linda & G-I Joe

Garrett:
You are such a special little boy
and everyone loves you & thinks
you are <u>so cool</u>! I remember
2 years ago when you showed me
your room. You were so sweet
to me & I've never forgotten how
big a hug you gave me when I
was leaving to go home. You make
<u>others</u> feel loved + special —
that's a great gift! We love you
very very much!
xxxooo

From his home on the other side of the moon, Father Time summoned eight of his most trusted storytellers to bring a message of hope to all children. Their mission was to spread magical tales throughout the world: tales that remind us that we all belong to one family, one world; that our hearts speak the same language, no matter where we live or how different we look or sound; and that we each have the right to be loved, to be nurtured, and to reach for a dream.

This is one of their stories.
Listen with your heart and share the magic.

FOR SYLVIE AND
HER UNCLE RICK,
WHOSE CAPACITY
TO LOVE HAS
AWAKENED OUR
HEARTS.

Our thanks to artists Shanna Grotenhuis, Jane Portaluppi, and Mindi Sarko,
as well as Sharon Beckett, Yoshie Brady, Andrea Cascardi, Solveig Chandler, Jun Deguchi,
Akiko Eguchi, Liz Gordon, Tetsuo Ishida, William Levy, Michael Lynton, Masaru Nakamura,
Steve Ouimet, Tomoko Sato, Isamu Senda, Minoru Shibuya, Jan Smith, and Hideaki Suda.

THE ENCHANTED TREE

An Original American Tale

Flavia Weedn & Lisa Weedn Gilbert

Illustrated by Flavia Weedn

Hyperion • New York

Once upon a time, in a small village surrounded by a
lush forest, there lived a pink giraffe. She was very pink
and very tall—in fact, she was the pinkest and the tallest
giraffe in her entire village, and she didn't like being so
different. She would often bend down and pretend she was
just like the other giraffes, but no matter how hard she
tried, she could never be anyone other than who she was,
and this made her sad. The pink giraffe wished she were
prettier and more graceful, but more than anything, she
just wanted to look like everyone else.

One day she decided to leave her village and take a long journey into the forest, in hopes that she could somehow learn how to change the way she looked. She believed this would make her life happier.

For many days and many nights she walked. Finally she grew so tired, she stopped to rest under a beautiful old tree, and soon the pink giraffe fell asleep. She slept for a very long time, then all at once, she was awakened by a voice. "Wake up, my friend, wake up!"

The giraffe quickly opened her eyes and sat up. She could hardly believe it, but it sounded as though the voice was coming from the tree. "Is that you, tree?" she asked. "Is that you talking?"

"Yes, it is me," answered the tree.

"But how can you speak? You are just a tree," said the pink giraffe. She had never heard a tree talk before, and she was very puzzled.

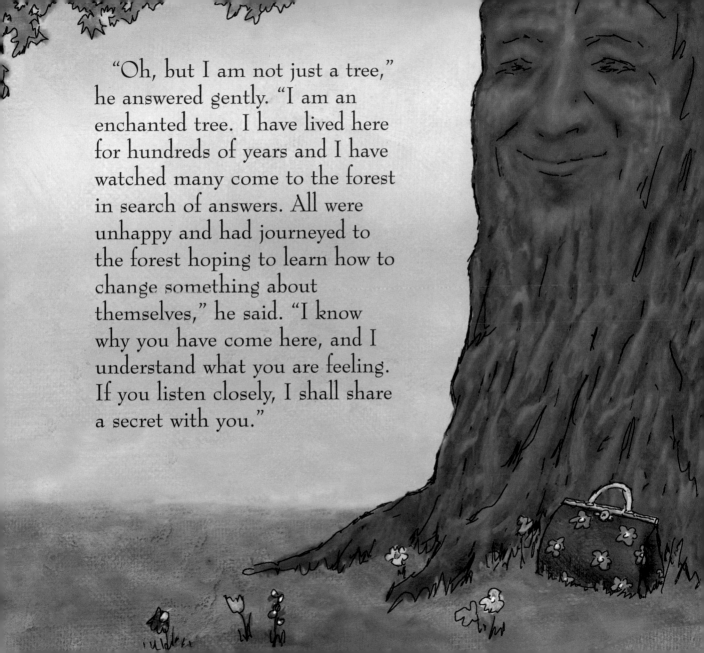

"Oh, but I am not just a tree," he answered gently. "I am an enchanted tree. I have lived here for hundreds of years and I have watched many come to the forest in search of answers. All were unhappy and had journeyed to the forest hoping to learn how to change something about themselves," he said. "I know why you have come here, and I understand what you are feeling. If you listen closely, I shall share a secret with you."

The pink giraffe was indeed in search of answers, so she paid close attention to the enchanted tree as he spoke.

"The first to come to me was an owl, who was very sad," said the tree. "He was a large owl, with beautiful lavender wings and shiny golden glasses. He was the only owl in his village who wore glasses, and he didn't like being different. Because he was an owl, he would sleep the entire day, and then at night he would stay awake to guard the forest and all the animals who lived there. He liked being one of the caretakers of the forest, but in order to see clearly and do his job well, he had to wear his glasses. All of the others in his village could see perfectly, and the owl wanted to be just like them."

"So I asked the owl to set aside his worries for a moment," said the tree, "and to tell me what he loved most about the night, what beautiful sights he saw, and how good it made him feel to protect the forest. The owl was quiet for a time, and then he spoke:

"'I love the moon and the sparkling fireflies that fill the night air,' the owl told me. 'I love reading bedtime stories to the tiny squirrels and watching them fall asleep peacefully, knowing that I am here to protect them. And I also love how the rising sun lets me know that morning is on its way by creating a beautiful, shimmering reflection of a rainbow in the corner of my glasses.'

"'Could you see all of this before you wore glasses?' I asked. 'Well, no,' the owl answered. 'Before I wore glasses everything I saw was fuzzy and unclear. I could never read stories to the squirrels and I never, ever, saw the reflection of a rainbow.'

"Through his glasses, the owl looked up at me," said the enchanted tree, "and a smile came over his face. As we spoke, he had learned what mattered most was that he could see, and being able to see was a wonderful gift.

"Only by wearing his glasses could he experience this gift, and it really wasn't important that he was the only one who wore them. In fact, he realized that being different from all of the other owls made him special and unique. Never before had he looked at himself in this way, and it made him feel very good inside.

"Other owls from his village heard our conversation and flew upon my branches to share their views. The owl listened to them, and he learned that because he wore glasses, he was the only one who ever saw a rainbow with the morning sunrise, and he was the only owl who ever read stories to the squirrels. He also learned that he was loved and respected by all who lived in his village, and this, too, made the owl feel special," said the enchanted tree.

"When our talk had finished, the owl flew away so much happier than when he had come to me. He had learned that he was perfect just the way he was—and from what I hear, he is now considered the wisest owl in the forest."

The pink giraffe liked this story, and she listened carefully as the enchanted tree continued.

"Later there came a turtle who rested against my trunk," said the enchanted tree. "The turtle was crying because she could not dance or jump or run like the other turtles. She was very small and slow, and she was very unhappy. She wanted to be larger and quicker, like the others in her village.

"We spoke for a time," said the tree, "and I asked her to try to think of what it was like being small. At first, the turtle was silent, but then she began to remember.

"Because she was small, she was able to walk very close to the ground. And because she walked so slowly, she could see all of the little ants, their villages, and the other wonderful creatures that lived in the tall grass. She was the first to see the beautiful colors of the tiniest flowers as they sprang up from the ground.

"I asked her if the other turtles could see these things and the turtle replied, 'Well, no. I am the only one small enough to see them. The others take larger steps and rush by me. I suppose they never see the beauty I see.' Upon saying this, the turtle smiled happily, for she suddenly realized that being small was actually very special."

The enchanted tree looked tenderly into the eyes of the pink giraffe and continued. "She realized that it was okay to be exactly who she was. In fact, it was a very wonderful thing to be the smallest turtle in her village. And as the turtle left the forest, I saw her smiling at the tiny ants who made their trails beneath the tall blades of grass, and I even saw her dance with the small flowers that brushed against her feet."

The pink giraffe sighed sadly and looked up at the enchanted tree. "I appreciate your help, enchanted tree, but I am different from these other animals," she said. "I do not wear glasses and I am certainly not too slow or too short.

"I am unhappy because I am too pink and too tall, and I feel so very awkward and unbeautiful."

"But you have a choice, dear giraffe, and you can choose to be proud of who you are, to find all the beauty within you, and to never be unhappy again," said the enchanted tree.

"But how?" asked the giraffe.

"That is the secret, my friend. It's all a matter of changing your mind and opening your heart to the good things in your life," answered the tree, for he was so very wise. "You, too, can do this, if you set aside your worries and listen deeply with your heart."

And so the pink giraffe nestled against the enchanted tree and listened even more closely as he continued to speak.

"Because you are tall, you can see over all of the trees and into the neighboring villages. Can any of the other giraffes do this?" the tree asked.

"Well, no," said the giraffe. "Even though I try to hide it, I am by far the tallest giraffe in my village. In fact, because I am the tallest I am often asked to stretch out my long neck and describe to the others what I see."

"Now close your eyes and imagine all the favorite things you see. Can you describe them to me?" asked the enchanted tree.

The pink giraffe took a moment, closed her eyes, and then she spoke. "Well, I like being the first to see the beautiful sunrise in the morning and the trail of songbirds that fly into the dew-covered treetops. I like being the only one who can see far into the distance, over the forest, and into the neighboring villages. I like feeling so close to the sky and to the moon and the stars that twinkle in the night," said the giraffe, pausing briefly to collect her thoughts.

"I understand that you're trying to make me see that it is not a bad thing to be taller, and I suppose you're right," said the pink giraffe. "There are a lot of very good things I am able to experience because I am tall. But, enchanted tree, my long legs and my tall neck make me look so different from all the other giraffes, and I'm so tired of trying to hide it. It makes me feel clumsy and awkward, and my knees ache from bending and my neck hurts from hunching over. And besides, I am so very pink! Not only am I the tallest giraffe, I'm the *only* pink giraffe in my whole village!"

The enchanted tree just smiled, leaned toward the pink giraffe, and said, "Have you ever thought that being pink means that you are the same beautiful color as a summer's evening and the sunsets that rise above the mountains and the trees? Have you ever noticed that you are the same soft hue as the fragrant tea roses and the blossoms on the fruit trees?" asked the enchanted tree. "And have you ever stopped to think that the only time you feel awkward and clumsy is when you are stooping down, trying to be shorter, pretending to be something you are not? Oh, dear giraffe, you are so stunning and beautiful, and you have so many gifts. Can't you see that you are very special just the way you are?"

The pink giraffe had been listening to the tree all along, but only now did she finally understand his message. The enchanted tree was right. The pink giraffe really was special because she was unlike any other giraffe.

"Oh, thank you, enchanted tree," she said. "Now I understand that we are all meant to be different, and because we are different we are each perfect in our own special way. I will always remember what you have taught me and I shall never forget the secret you have shared."

Then the giraffe hugged the tree and began her journey back home.

And just like all the others who had stopped to rest beside the enchanted tree before her, the pink giraffe left smiling. Now, instead of being sad, the pink giraffe was filled with joy, for she understood the secret. She stretched her long neck out as far as she could, stood high and proud and strong, and looked up at the sky happily. Never again would she try to hide who she was, for she was exactly who she was supposed to be. She was the tallest and the pinkest giraffe in her village, and from this day on, she would never want to be anything or anyone else.

The enchanted tree looked on with love as he watched the pink giraffe leave the forest. His heart filled with pride, knowing that the beautiful secret . . . the secret of loving who you are . . . had once again made a sad heart become a happy one. The enchanted tree's branches seemed to sparkle with joy.

And instead of walking, the pink giraffe danced all the way home.

Produced in cooperation with Dream Maker Studios AG.
Printed in Singapore.
For information address Hyperion Books for Children,
114 Fifth Avenue, New York, New York 10011.

FIRST EDITION
1 3 5 7 9 10 8 6 4 2

Library of Congress Cataloging-in-Publication Data

Weedn, Flavia
The enchanted tree/Flavia Weedn & Lisa Weedn Gilbert;
illustrated by Flavia Weedn—1st ed.
p. cm.—(Flavia dream maker stories)
Summary: A very tall, very pink giraffe is ashamed to be so different
from the other giraffes in the forest, until an enchanted tree helps her see
that she is perfect just the way she is.
ISBN 0-7868-0120-4
[1. Giraffes—Fiction. 2. Self–acceptance—Fiction.]
I. Gilbert, Lisa Weedn. II. Title.
III. Series: Weedn, Flavia. Flavia dream maker stories.
PZ7.W4145En   1995
[E]—dc20   94–32813

The artwork for each picture is digitally mastered using acrylic on canvas.
This book is set in 17-point Bernhard Modern.